Jack's House

BY **Karen Magnuson Beil**

ILLUSTRATED BY
Mike Wohnoutka

Holiday House / New York

3 5 7 9 10 8 6 4

Library of Congress Cataloging-in-Publication Data
Beil, Karen Magnuson.
Jack's house / by Karen Magnuson Beil ; illustrated by Mike Wohnoutka. — 1st ed.
p. cm.
Summary: Cumulative text reveals who was really responsible for the house that
Jack claims to have built, and all of the trucks involved, from the bulldozer used
to clear the land to the van that brought a hammock for the backyard.
ISBN 978-0-8234-1913-5 (hardcover)
[1. Building—Fiction. 2. Trucks—Fiction. 3. Dwellings—Fiction. 4. Dogs—Fiction.
5. Humorous stories.] I. Wohnoutka, Mike, ill. II. Title.
PZ7.B3882349Jac 2008
[E]—dc22
2007014978

ISBN 978-0-8234-2242-5 (pbk)
HOLIDAY HOUSE is registered in the U.S. Patent and Trademark Office.

For Kirsten
with love
K. M. B.

For Franklin,
who digs trucks
M. W.

This is Jack.

And this is the house
that Jack said he built.
But here is the real story—
and pictures to prove it.

This is the bulldozer
that scraped the land
for Jack's house.

This is the backhoe
that dug the cellar
where the land was scraped
for Jack's house.

This is the cement mixer
that poured the floor
where the cellar was dug
where the land was scraped
for Jack's house.

This is the forklift
that hoisted bricks to build the walls
where the floor was poured
where the cellar was dug
where the land was scraped
for Jack's house.

This is the rack truck
that delivered windows to let in light
where the walls were bricked
where the floor was poured
where the cellar was dug
where the land was scraped
for Jack's house.

This is the boom truck
that raised the shingles to the roof
where the windows were framed
where the walls were bricked
where the floor was poured
where the cellar was dug
where the land was scraped
for Jack's house.

This is the dump truck
that hauled two trees to shade the house
where the roof was nailed
where the windows were framed
where the walls were bricked
where the floor was poured
where the cellar was dug
where the land was scraped
for Jack's house.

This is the van
that brought the hammock, cozy and snug,
where the trees were planted
and the roof was nailed
and the windows were framed
and the walls were bricked
and the floor was poured
and the cellar was dug
and the land was scraped
for Jack's house.

This is Jack
relaxing out back.

This is the dog
who did all the work.

And this is the pickup truck . . .

that carried away a patch of grass,
two trees,
the hammock,
and Jack.

This is the house that *Max* built.